On the edge

Up For It

Trevor Millum

Folens

© 2003 Folens Limited, on behalf of the author.

United Kingdom: Folens Publishers, Apex Business Centre, Boscombe Road, Dunstable, LU5 4RL.
Email: folens@folens.com

Ireland: Folens Publishers, Greenhills Road, Tallaght, Dublin 24.
Email: info@folens.ie

Poland: JUKA, ul. Renesansowa 38, Warsaw 01-905.

Editor: Kay Macmullan
Layout artist: Suzanne Ward
Cover design: Duncan McTeer

First published 2003 by Folens Limited.

British Library Cataloguing in Publication Data. A catalogue record for this publication is available from the British Library.

ISBN 1 84303 397–6

Contents

The story so far

If you haven't read an *On the edge* book before:
The stories take place in and around a row of shops and buildings called Pier Parade in Brightsea, right next to the sea. There's Big Fry, the fish and chip shop; Drop Zone, the drop-in centre for local teenagers; Macmillan's, the sweet and souvenir shop; Anglers' Haven, the fishing tackle shop; the Surf 'n' Skate shop and, of course, the Brightsea Beach Bar.

If you have read an *On the edge* book you may have met these people before.

Vicki Johnson: *lives with her parents at the fish and chip shop; goes to college.*

Will Page: *goes to college in the town.*

So, what's been going on?
Everyone knows that Vicki doesn't stay with one boyfriend for long, she soon gets bored and moves on. Has she chosen sensibly this time though?

What happens in this story?
Vicki goes with Will to a meet on North End beach, and although she finds the car racing can be exciting, she's not prepared for all it involves.

1

Ride home

"Wanna lift?"
She looked down.
She knew the face.
"Who's asking?"
"Mac."
"Mac who?"
"Mac yer bloody mind up!"

She told him to push off and
walked away.

The car took off with a squeal.
The exhaust fumes hit her face.
She swore at the driver – but without any
real venom.
At the traffic lights she saw him again.
Impatient.
Nothing he could do about the line
of traffic.

The seafront was always busy at this
time of day.
'Tough luck, boy racer!' she said
to herself.
She crossed the seafront at the
pelican crossing.
Half-way across the road she heard a
car horn.
A head poked out of a different car.
"Hey, Vicki!"
It was Will, a guy from college.
She waved.

"Get in!" he called.
The car behind hooted.
Will gave it a sign.
"Don't," said Vicki, "he'll get road rage."
"Nah. They're always like that."
But the car hooted again.
"Come on. Get in, then," said Will.

She shrugged, pulled open the door and
climbed in.
It shut with a clang.
Will let out the clutch and the car
leapt away.

"Let me get the belt on!" she cried. "You nearly had me through the windscreen."

He just grinned.

"Must be my unlucky day," she said. " You're the second one to offer me a lift."

"Who was the first?"

"I dunno – seen him about. Mac or something. Didn't like the look of him."

Will smiled to himself.

Vicki was in between boyfriends.
Will wasn't ideal – but he was OK.
Better than being on her own.

Two nights ago she'd told Tony not to call her for a few days.
He was getting too serious.
He had money and a car.
But that wasn't everything.
Her mum and dad liked him – and that was worrying.

"There's a meet at North End," said Will.

"A few of us are going up."

"A what?"

"You know – just a bit of fun. All the guys with wheels will be there."

She looked around the car.
It was a wreck.
"You got a handicap?"

"Yeah – this motor." He laughed. "It's not that organised. There's no guy with a flag! Just showing off, tricks. You know."

Another set of lights changed.
The car leapt away again.
They were on the dual carriageway now.
Will could get away fast but now they were on a straight road and other cars started passing them.

"Looks like you need a sprint, not a long distance," said Vicki.

"Yeah, well, any fool can drive fast. You just stick your foot down and keep it there."

She had never thought of it like that before.

"You drive?" he said.

"No. Always got someone to drive me." She smiled – like a film star, she hoped. It wasn't true, of course. She was quite used to walking or getting the bus. The odd times when she used a taxi she shared it with others. Once she'd call a cab – on her own!

She sighed. In the meantime, here she was in a beat-up car with a guy in a baseball cap. Will would have to do for now.

2

Beach race

The North End beach was a great place.
It was three miles from Brightsea, in a
quiet town, full of retirement homes
and bungalows.
In the daytime in summer there were
camper vans, cars and even coaches.
Most would be people just looking at
the sea.
Some would drive there, eat their
sandwiches, read the paper and then
drive home.
Not even get out of the car.

Now, at 10 o'clock in the evening, out of
season, it was deserted – two miles of
clear tarmac just for them.
Until the cops came – and they were
never there on time!

The main road ran alongside.
It curved above the North End beach and
then into the town, or you could swing
round the one-way traffic system and
head back towards Brightsea.

They turned off and headed towards a
group of headlights.
There were five cars there already.
Vicki saw Mac standing by one of them.
There were a couple of newer-looking
Fords, a Peugeot, even an old Audi – and
a Vauxhall even older than Will's.
All the engines were running.

Will got out and went over to one of the
other drivers.
She stayed where she was and
watched him.
Was this really where she wanted to be on
a Friday night?
For a moment she wished that she
could drive.

Vicki looked out at the sea.
In the fading light she could make out the
waves breaking on the shingle.

She heard doors slam and engines rev.
Two of the cars edged forward.
Then, with a noise as if from a film set,
they roared away.
The remaining figures stood watching.
There was not much talking.
There was not much to say.

Will came back to the car and got in.

"Why do tyres make that noise?"
asked Vicki.

"What noise?"

"You know, that squealing noise. When
you start off too fast."

He thought about it.
"I dunno," he said. "They just do."
He reversed and turned the car.

He wound down the window and they both sat looking up the stretch of tarmac. The red rear lights had disappeared.

"What are we looking at?"

"They'll be back. They turn at the roundabout."

As he spoke, the headlights showed. The sound of the engines came next. One car was ahead – but not by much. Vicki didn't feel safe. She wanted to get out and scramble up the slope. But she knew she couldn't. They sat and watched as the cars shot past. There were some shouts but no one cheered.

"They're a miserable lot," she said. Will said nothing.

A short distance behind them, the cars slowed and turned. The drivers exchanged some banter.

Then a face appeared at the
open window.
It was Mac – or whatever he
called himself.
"Ready?" he grunted.

"Ready," said Will.

Vicki realised that a contest had been
agreed earlier.
Now, like it or not, she was part of it.

This time there were three cars.
Vicki didn't notice any signal and she
gasped as Will took his foot off the clutch.
The old Ford leapt forward.
Will went through the gears like butter.
For the first half-mile they were in front.
Then the power of Mac's Peugeot began
to pay off.
It edged ahead.
The third car was gaining too.

But then there were the Stop signs.
The main road was beyond – and
the roundabout.

Vicki didn't want to think about
the traffic.
She just hoped there wasn't any.

Mac slowed so suddenly they nearly hit
his rear wing.
Will cursed, braked and followed him
round the kerb.

Then they were facing back along the
beach road.
Will was in the lead again, coming fast off
the roundabout.
Vicki rocked against the door as the
car cornered.
Then she swayed into Will as he
straightened up for the sprint back.

Mac was on their tail again.
Will kept his foot down but there was
nothing more he could do.
Any fool can drive fast, she remembered.

The Peugeot was alongside.
Vicki looked out of her window.

She looked into the grinning face of
the driver.
Then he pulled ahead.
The third car was close behind, but the
race was as good as over.

Vicki breathed out.
She had been holding her breath,
without noticing.
So, yeah, it was exciting.
In a way.

When they stopped, she wanted to get out.
But she had nothing to say to
these people.
There was only one other girl, and she
had no desire to start a conversation
with her.
She wanted a drink – and she wanted
someone to buy it for her.
Suddenly, she wanted someone with a
large, warm car and a bit of money.
She thought about Tony.
She looked at Will.
Oh well.

Will didn't push his luck.
He drove her home – well, to the road
above the chip shop.

"We've got a bet on tomorrow," he said.

"Yeah?"

"Me and that Mac. Only twenty quid.
He's bringing a passenger."

"I thought you said there wasn't much
racing. Just tricks and stuff."

"Well, there is. But this isn't a proper
cruise. This is me and Mac. Sort of
personal. I need to get some better wheels
before I turn up for a cruise."

Vicki thought about it.
She'd make Will work hard for this.

"And why are you telling me all this?"

"Well, it'll be fair, won't it? The weight
will be the same in each car."

She still looked blank.

"That's if you'll be in mine …"

Will looked like an expectant puppy.
Albeit a dangerous one.
Should she throw him a bone to chew?

Vicki was about to say 'In your dreams!'
but she stopped.
What else would she be doing
tomorrow night?
Filing her nails?
Washing her hair?
Helping in the chip shop?

In the end, she nodded.
"All right. But meet me here – not outside
the shop."

"Pick you up at nine," he said.
He drove off – quietly.
She gave him extra points for that.

3

Question time

"Where are you off to?" asked her mum.

"I'm out with Will," she said.

"What happened to Tony?"

Her mum had virtually given up trying to work out Vicki's love life.
After the business in the summer with those students from the language school, she knew better than to pry too deeply.
And Phil, Vicki's brother, kept well clear.

"He's resting," she said, eventually, smiling to herself.

Her mum looked puzzled but didn't ask
what she meant.
"And who's this Will? Is that his
real name?"

"Oh just a bloke I know. Friend of Gaz's."

"And where are you going?"

"Just for a drive … Nothing serious."

"So he's got a car too, eh?" said Ken, her
step-dad, who had been listening.

"Mmm," she replied.
She didn't want to let on what a wreck
it was.

The shop bell rang.
Her mum went off to serve the customer.
"How long has he been driving?"
asked Ken.

"I don't know. But he's a good driver."

"I've never met anyone who said they were a bad driver," was all Ken said. Just before she left, he asked "Got your mobile?"

"Of course."

"Leave it switched on – we'll both feel happier knowing we can contact you."

Vicki thought about this.
It sounded like checking up on her, but there was no point alienating them.
It just caused trouble.

She nodded.
"OK. See you later. Bye, Mum."

She closed the door before more questions could be asked.

4

Return match

He was waiting at the corner.
She looked around.
Did she mind if anyone saw her?
Saw her getting into this old car?
Probably not – it was quite cool, in a way.

Will looked the same.
Black top, blue baseball cap.
Perhaps he hadn't taken his clothes off
since last night.

"Don't get the idea that I like this," she
said. "Being a weight handicap. It's not
my idea of a good night out."

He said nothing, just grinned.
She looked good.

"Meet Matt," he said, gesturing towards
the rear seat.
Matt was a sharp-faced lad of
about fourteen.
"My cousin," said Will.
Vicki thought she'd seen Matt down by
the Drop Zone on Pier Parade.

She was not pleased.
What kind of a date was this?
"Is he a handicap too?"

Will grinned again.
"No. He'll have to get out. He
doesn't mind."

'And she'll stay in. She doesn't mind,'
thought Vicki.

The car rattled away from another set
of lights.
Matt hadn't said a word.
He was listening to his MP3 player.
Where did he get the money for that?

Vicki made comments about the traffic,
asked questions about the car.
'I sound middle-aged,' she thought.
But she couldn't stand silences – so
she chattered.

Will made the odd remark.
He liked talking about the car.
He did his best to keep it running.
He had to beg and borrow parts to keep it
on the road.
He knew all the scrap yards
round Brightsea.
"MOT soon," he sighed. "Worse
than exams."

* * * * *

There were three cars there when
they arrived.
Mac's car was not among them.
This time Vicki got out and stood around
with the others.

Car radios thumped.
Lighters flared and flickered.
Not much was said.

Vicki looked at the sea.

Then she turned and looked up the steep slope to the main road.

A well-lit bus went by.

Beyond it she could just see the lights of the Man at Arms pub.

It looked inviting.

Engines were started and stopped.

Someone fiddled with battery leads.

There was a smell of oil and cheap aftershave.

One of the cars practised a spin, and everyone laughed when it stalled.

In the distance they could see the lights of the pier down the coast in Brightsea.

They looked inviting too.

"Here he is," said Will.

Matt looked up.

For the first time that evening, he looked interested.

The Peugeot drove up noisily.

The loud exhaust was deliberate.

A girl sat in the passenger seat.
'I've seen her somewhere,' said Vicki
to herself.
She couldn't think where.
Behind a bar perhaps.

Mac didn't get out.
"Ready for a thrashing?" was all he said.

Will said nothing.
The doors of the car hung open.
He climbed in, slammed the door and
revved the engine.
Vicki got in the other side.
It took two tries to shut the door.

The cars sat side by side.
Both drivers tried to look casual.

There was an invisible signal.
The growl of the engines became a roar.

They jerked forward before she
was ready.

But this time Will was too keen.
His take-off was too quick and the car
wheels spun before they could grip.
They lost valuable seconds.
They were only half-way towards the
roundabout when the Peugeot overtook.
Vicki did not look at the driver or
his passenger.
Will stared ahead.

Mac took the roundabout like a
hairpin bend.
Will was still heading towards it when
the Peugeot started back towards them.
The headlamps glared at them, undipped.
Will screeched round, clipping the
kerb twice.
He wasn't driving well.
Vicki clutched the door handle and held
her breath.
But there was no catching Mac now.

She willed the car to go faster, willed
Mac's car to swerve and stutter to a halt.
Neither of these happened.
She was surprised how disappointed
she felt.

When they pulled up, Mac was already standing by his car, hand out.

Will fished out a grubby note, leant out of the window and passed it to him.

"Easy money," said Mac, grinning. "I'm not sitting around with losers. We're off to the Man. Coming?"
He meant the Man at Arms.

Will shook his head.
He had no money – and anyway,
Mac was the last person he wanted to drink with.
Mac shrugged, climbed back into the car and screeched off.

Will sat silently, hands gripping the steering wheel.
His knuckles looked white.
Vicki felt sorry for him.
"You didn't really expect to beat him, did you?" she asked. "Anyway, he's a loser," she said with as much conviction as possible.
She wasn't terribly convincing.

"Nah, I'm the loser," said Will.

Then he seemed to snap out of it.
He jumped out of the car, and lit
a cigarette.
Matt wandered over.
Will handed him the cigarette and he took
a couple of drags.
"Tough," he said.
That was all.
Better than nothing, thought Vicki.

Two of the other cars set off down
the strip.
Will and Vicki leant against the side of the
car, listening to music from the
green Vauxhall.
They kept an eye out for police cars,
but no one seemed bothered about
them tonight.
A couple of lights went on in the
bungalows on the other side of the
seafront, but Vicki knew no one would
come out.

Someone might make a phone call, but
they'd be long gone.

The music from the radio paused and a
DJ spoke.
Then, for a moment it was quiet.

Clang! Clink!

Vicki spun round in time to see a can
rolling on the tarmac.
It had bounced off the car roof.
She looked closer – it was a lager can.

Will looked cross.
They stared up the slope.
Then there was another can.
It missed the car – but there was the
sound of laughter.
Did they hear – or just imagine – the
word "Loser"?

"The Man at Arms is just at the top
there," said Vicki. "I can't see who's
there ..."

It was too dark to see anyone – but they
knew who it was.

The pub was situated at the top of a scrubby bit of hill at the end of the seafront where they were parked. They were almost underneath it.

Will looked lost for a moment.
Then he turned to Matt.

"Come on," he said to him. "Let's take a look."
He reached under the dashboard and took something out.

"Don't be stupid," said Vicki, alarmed.

"It's all right," said Will, holding up the tyre gauge. "Just going to check his tyres. Mac's tyres seemed pretty low to me. Don't want him having an accident."

"You've changed your tune," said Vicki. "Thought you hated the guy. Besides it's probably him lobbing cans at us."

"No point in holding grudges," said Will, beginning to walk away from the car.

5

Tyre service

Matt and Will started up the steps that led
to the main road.
They kept in the shadows where
they could.
It was a long way but they were in
no hurry.

They reached the top.
Will peered out from behind the
low hedge.
There was no one about.

They walked over to the pub, searching
for the Peugeot.
It wasn't in the small car park.
Will swore.
"They've left already," he grunted.
Matt said nothing.
Then he pulled Will's arm and pointed.

The car was on the road, half-hidden by
a white van.

They moved towards it.
"Keep a look out," said Will.
He bent to the tyre, found the dust cap
and removed it.
There was a hiss as he fitted the
tyre gauge.
He held it so that the air escaped.

Will looked round.
"Let's go."

Matt stayed where he was.
"They can just change one wheel," he
said. "That don't mean anything."

Will nodded.
"Yeah. You're right. One tyre could have
been chance. I want them to know it
was me."

He bent down again.
This time the valve was hard to find in
the dark.

The cap was tricky to move.
Everything was difficult.
Then he had it.
The nice hiss of escaping air!

For good measure, Matt picked up a stone
and scraped it along the side of
the Peugeot.
It made a long, jagged, silver scar.

"Cut it out!" said Will.
But it was too late.
Matt chucked the stone away.

Then he heard footsteps.
It was Mac!
Matt shot across the road.
Will followed.
There were shouts.

Where was the gap in the hedge?
Will couldn't see where the steps started.
He wasn't going to wait around.
It sounded as if Mac had friends
with him.

He jumped over the hedge.
Matt was close behind.

It was a steep slope.

Neither of them could stop sliding down
the grass.
They tried to get a grip and then lost it.
There were bushes here and there.

Will reached out.
He grabbed a branch.
Thorns bit into his hand.
He swore and let go.

6

Playing ambulances

By the car, Vicki was fed up.
Everyone else had gone.
Someone had even offered her a lift.
She should have said yes.
If she'd been able to drive, she would
have taken the car and gone home.
Idiots!
Typical bloody boys.
Boys with toys.
The worst combination.

She thought of walking back to town.
She could get a bus from the main road.
She thought of calling Tony.
She even had the phone in her hand when
she heard the noises.
She looked up.

Something was rolling down the slope.
What the hell was it?
Were they sending beer barrels
down now?
There were two of them.

Then she realised.
It was Will and Matt.
What were they playing at?
They'd kill themselves!

They half-fell, half-rolled down the rest
of the slope.
A pain shot through Will's elbow where
he hit something hard.
Then they were almost at the bottom.
The last few metres were soft – and then
there was a drop, down on to the tarmac.
They hit the ground within seconds of
each other.

Vicki ran over to them.
They lay in the light of the headlamps.

Matt tried to get up and then fell
back, yelling.

She was relieved to see Will stand up
– but then he staggered and leant against
the wall.

"I can't stand properly," gasped Will.
"My knee. And my elbow's killing me."

'I do not want to see bones sticking
through flesh,' thought Vicki.
"Lean on me," she said.
Will limped to the car.
He slumped into the driver's seat.
"Get Matt," he said.

She went back to where Matt was sitting.
She helped him up.
His leg seemed even worse.
She had to half-carry him to the car and
lay him on the back seat.
He'd stopped yelling and gone very pale.

She got into the passenger seat.

"I can't drive," said Will. "I just tried … I
can't do anything with my left arm."

"Let's get help, then," said Vicki. "Let's call an ambulance."

Will looked at her.
He looked scared.
"With Mac and his friends on their way?
Wait for an ambulance?"

Vicki looked at him.
She should have known.
As if Will was really going to help
Mac out!
How could she have been so dumb?
She thought, not for the first time that
evening, 'What am I doing here?'

She said, "I can change gear. You drive.
Just tell me when. You can steer with one
arm, can't you?"

He nodded.

He put his foot on the clutch and swore.
"That hurts! All right. Now – first gear
– yes!"

He removed his left foot from the clutch and jammed his right foot on the accelerator.
The car leapt away.

"Second! Straight back – yeah, that's it …"
He breathed out in pain.
The engine roared – too loud.

"Third is towards the front and over to the right. Now."

There was a grinding noise.
She tried again and got the same noise.
Then she found it.
They gathered speed.

"I hope they're not waiting at the roundabout," she said.

"Me too."

Neither had any idea what Mac and his mates could do.
Put up a road block?
Not with his car.

And there hadn't been time to organise anyone else.

Surely they wouldn't stand in the road?

The beach road was still deserted.
With difficulty, Will turned up on to the main road.

"Back to second," he said.

Immediately a line of cars appeared behind them.
They were only doing thirty.
It was all they could manage
between them.
Several cars hooted.
Will couldn't even manage a V sign.

The car staggered on.

"We'd better get you to A and E," said Vicki, trying to remember the way.

"A and E?"

"Accident and Emergency. Casualty. Whatever."

He didn't argue.
The pain in his leg was getting worse.
He could hardly bear to put his
foot down.

"I should be able to change gear without
the clutch," he said. "Just needs to be the
right revs."

She didn't know what he was
talking about.
"Just tell me what to do," she said.

The car gained speed.
"Now," he said.
She slid the gear lever into fourth as if
she'd been doing it for years.
They sped towards town.
Vicki looked into the back.
Matt was staring back at her.
There were beads of sweat on his face.

He even smiled – in a pained way.
He can't be too bad, she thought.

Each time they came towards traffic
lights, she prayed they'd turn to green
before they got there.

They judged it as best they could.
The worst time was when they had to
stop and they needed first gear.
Will had to brace himself for the pain of
pushing down the clutch pedal.
Once they were moving, they could
manage without – just about.

Vicki's geography wasn't that good.
They took two wrong turnings.
Then she saw the signs.
'A & E'.
"Nearly there," she said.
She glanced over her shoulder.
Matt's eyes were closed.
"Not long now," she said.
She spoke to herself as much as
to anyone.
Then, they were shuddering to a halt.
They drew up where it said
'Ambulances Only'.

She walked round to the driver's door.

She opened it and held out an arm.
Will leant on her gratefully.

He had to shuffle round to get on her
right side.
Then he hopped and hobbled up
the ramp.
Someone came towards them.
Someone who knew what to do.
A wheelchair appeared.
Will fell into it.

"There's another one in the car," she said.
"Another person, I mean."
She couldn't think of the word 'casualty'.

She felt very tired.
She looked at her watch.
It was only half past ten.

Matt was fetched from the car.
She watched Matt and Will as they spoke
to the nurse.
They sat side by side in wheelchairs.
There was something comic about them.
"Boy racers!" Vicki said to herself.

7

Picking up

She'd been there for forty minutes before
she thought of phoning.
She thought of calling a taxi.
Then she thought of calling her mum.
She changed her mind again.
It was worth a try.
She reached for her mobile.

* * * * *

An orderly came up to her with the
car keys.

He told her that he'd moved the car.
She pointed at Will.
"He's the driver," she said.

The man looked at her in surprise.
"He drove here?"

She nodded.
"Sort of. With some help," she said.

She walked back outside and waited.
It began to rain and she let it wash over
her face.
Then she remembered where she was
– and who she was waiting for.
She rushed inside and found the toilets.
She did what she could to her hair and
her eyes.
Somewhere along the way she'd lost her
lip gloss, but she still looked good.
Well, fairly.

She looked in the mirror.
She had a moment of self-doubt.

Who was she?

She thought of those boyfriends – Mark,
Stefan, Will.
And the others.
Why did she bother with them?
She liked having them around.
More than girls.

Boys … men … were useless, but you couldn't do without them.
Perhaps it was the danger.
She knew that all the ones she'd liked had let her down in some way.
She'd liked something about Mac, too.
Despite his nasty side.
But she guessed she wouldn't be seeing him again.

When she came out, Matt and Will were still side by side.
Silent.

Their eyes followed her.

She walked to the door.
As she reached the ramp, a figure walked up.

"Tony!"

He took her arm.
"Are you all right?"

"I'm bloody glad to see you," she said, with feeling. "But I just need to say goodbye to my … to the patients."

She walked back over to Matt and Will. Someone had given them painkillers, but they clearly weren't working yet.
Matt was still wincing with pain.
Will looked ashen.
Behind them, a small girl was being wheeled by with her leg in plaster.

Matt and Will looked like little boys.
No older than the girl in the wheelchair.

"I'm off," she said. "It's been – um – interesting. Hope you're better soon."

Will looked at her.
"Thanks," he said.
Then, blinking, "How are we going to get home?"

"Phone a friend," she said.